anythink

anythink

# There Was a Tall Texan Who Swallowed a Flea

# There Was a Tall Texan Who Swallowed a Flea

By Susan Holt Kralovansky

Illustrated by Deborah Ousley Kadair

PELICAN PUBLISHING COMPANY
GRETNA 2013

*In memory of my father, George Holt,*
*who often overate in the Lone Star State—S. H. K.*

*Jamee, Krystal, and Patty—thanks for helping me stand tall!—D. O. K.*

*The word "Pelican" and the depiction of a pelican are*
*trademarks of Pelican Publishing Company, Inc., and are*
*registered in the U.S. Patent and Trademark Office.*

**Library of Congress Cataloging-in-Publication Data**

Kralovansky, Susan Holt.
  There was a tall Texan who swallowed a flea / Susan Holt Kralovansky ;
illustrated by Deborah Ousley Kadair.
       p. cm.
  Summary: In this variation on the traditional cumulative rhyme, a toad, a
snake, and a mockingbird are part of the feast for a rather unusual Texan.
    ISBN 978-1-4556-1717-3 (hardcover : alk. paper) — ISBN 978-1-4556-
1718-0 (e-book) 1. Folk songs, English—Texts. [1. Folk songs. 2. Nonsense
verses.] I. Kadair, Deborah Ousley, ill. II. Title.
  PZ8.3.K8613The 2013
  782.42—dc23
  [E]
                              2012024755

Printed in Malaysia
Published by Pelican Publishing Company, Inc.
1000 Burmaster Street, Gretna, Louisiana 70053

# THERE WAS A TALL TEXAN WHO SWALLOWED A FLEA

There was a tall Texan who swallowed a flea. It jumped on his knee, that silly old flea.

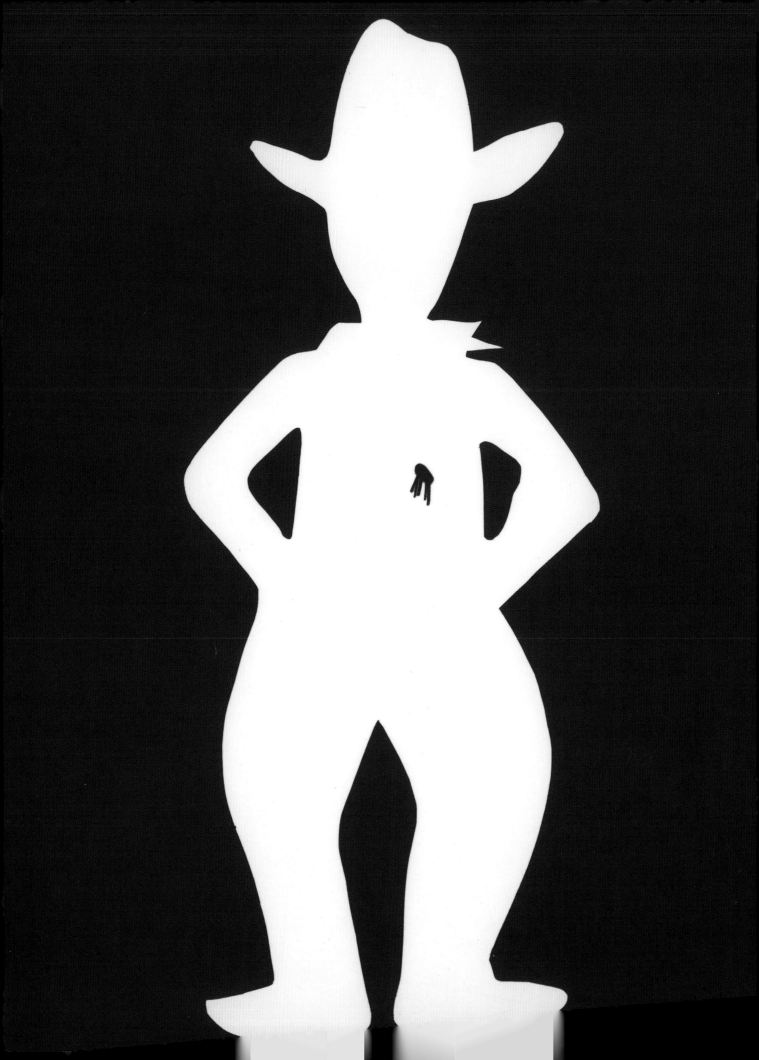

Whoo-ee! I can't believe he
swallowed a flea.

There was a tall Texan who swallowed a toad. He grabbed that toad right off the road.

He swallowed the toad to catch the flea. It jumped on his knee, that silly old flea.

Whoo-ee! I can't believe he swallowed a flea.

There was a tall Texan who swallowed a snake. It made him shake, that rattlin' snake.

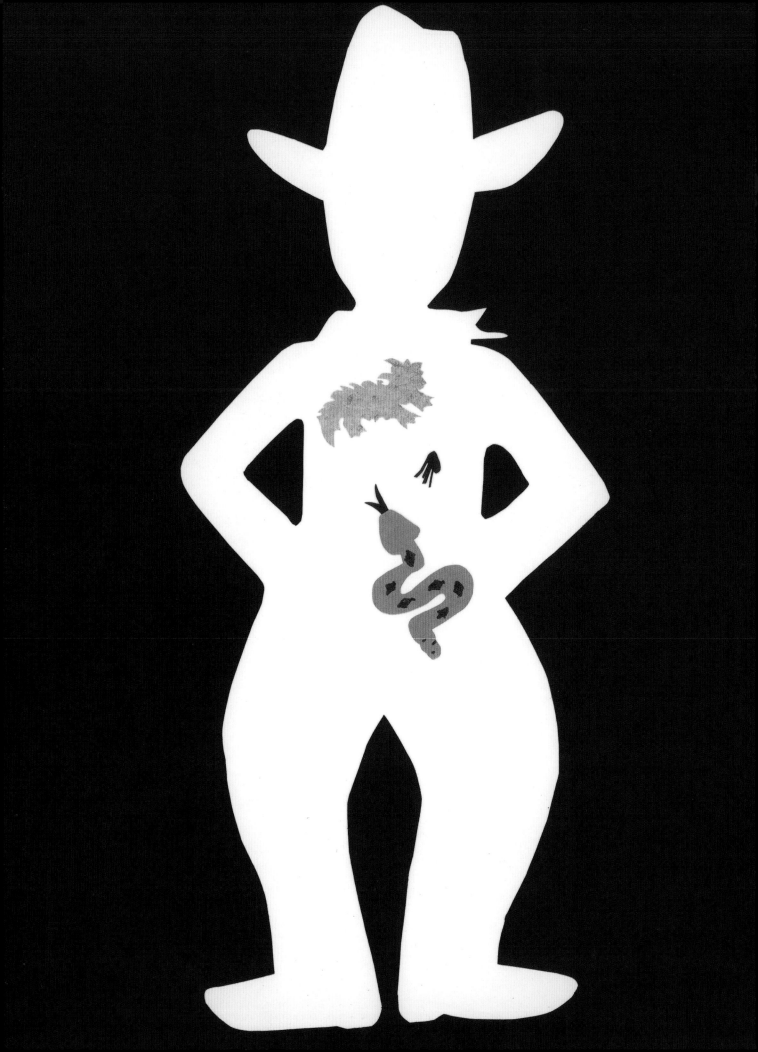

He swallowed the snake to eat the toad.

He swallowed the toad to catch the flea. It jumped on his knee, that silly old flea.

Whoo-ee! I can't believe he swallowed a flea.

There was a tall Texan who swallowed a bird—a mocking-bird, that's what I heard.

He swallowed the bird to scold the snake.

He swallowed the snake to eat the toad.

He swallowed the toad to catch the flea. It jumped on his knee, that silly old flea.

Whoo-ee! I can't believe he swallowed a flea.

There was a tall Texan
who swallowed a 'dillo, an
armadillo as big as a pillow.

He swallowed the 'dillo to shush the bird.

He swallowed the bird to scold the snake.

He swallowed the snake to eat the toad.

He swallowed the toad to catch the flea. It jumped on his knee, that silly old flea.

Whoo-ee! I can't believe he swallowed a flea.

There was a tall Texan who swallowed a bat. Imagine that, a free-tailed bat!

He swallowed the bat to bite the 'dillo.

He swallowed the 'dillo to shush the bird.

He swallowed the bird to scold the snake.

He swallowed the snake to eat the toad.

He swallowed the toad to catch the flea. It jumped on his knee, that silly old flea.

Whoo-ee! I can't believe he swallowed a flea.

There was a tall Texan who swallowed a boot. That crazy coot swallowed his boot!

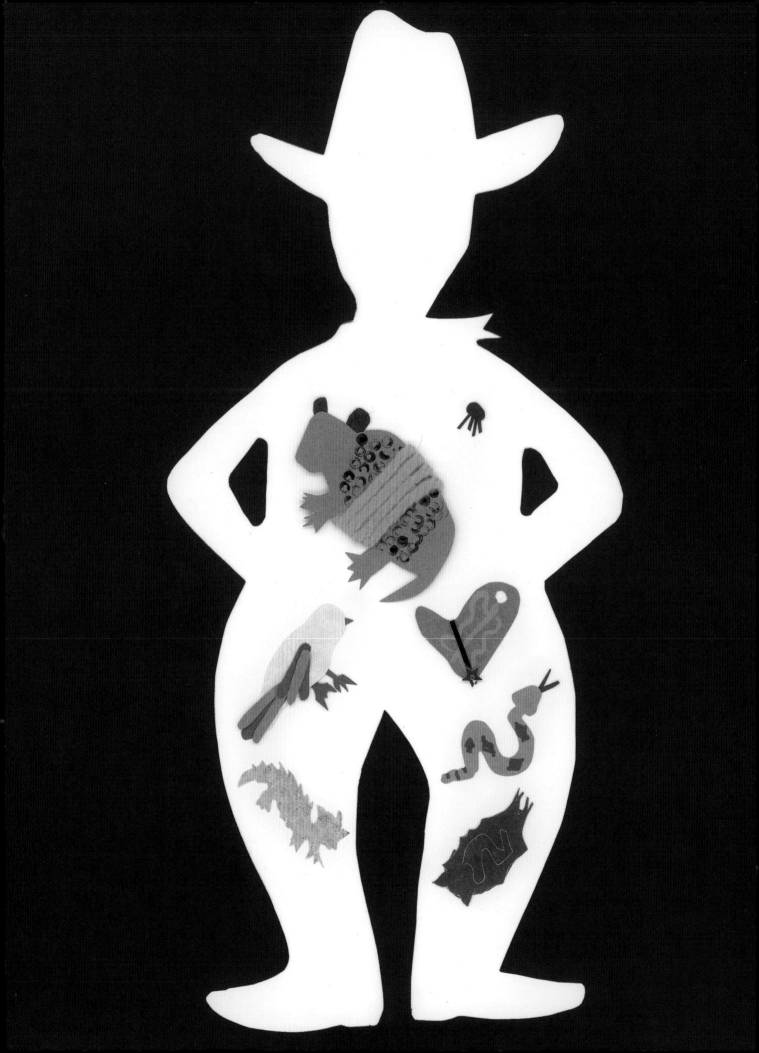

He swallowed the boot to stomp the bat.

He swallowed the bat to bite the 'dillo.

He swallowed the 'dillo to shush the bird.

He swallowed the bird to scold the snake.

He swallowed the snake to eat the toad.

He swallowed the toad to catch the flea. It jumped on his knee, that silly old flea.

Whoo-ee! I can't believe he swallowed a flea.

There was a tall Texan who swallowed a cactus. He practiced and practiced to swallow a cactus.

He swallowed the cactus to poke the boot.

He swallowed the boot to stomp the bat.

He swallowed the bat to bite the 'dillo.

He swallowed the 'dillo to shush the bird.

He swallowed the bird to scold the snake.

He swallowed the snake to eat the toad.

He swallowed the toad to catch the flea. It jumped on his knee, that silly old flea.

Whoo-ee! I can't believe he swallowed a flea.

There was a tall Texan who swallowed a bull. He thought he'd be full if he swallowed a bull.

He swallowed the bull to squish the cactus.

He swallowed the cactus to poke the boot.

He swallowed the boot to stomp the bat.

He swallowed the bat to bite the 'dillo.

He swallowed the 'dillo to shush the bird.

He swallowed the bird to scold the snake.

He swallowed the snake to eat the toad.

He swallowed the toad to catch the flea. It jumped on his knee, that silly old flea.

Whoo-ee! I can't believe he swallowed a flea.

There was a tall Texan
with a bad bellyache,
'cause he ate too much
in the Lone Star State.
Whoo-ee! All because
of a flea.